Welcome to the world of
LEGO® *Disney Princess*™! In this book you'll find
lots of stickers to create fantastic scenes.

You'll need pens and pencils
for coloring and drawing.

Use the stickers for the activities, too!

There's so much fun to be had in the
LEGO *Disney Princess* sticker world!

Use the stickers to create an incredible
scene at Cinderella's castle!

Stick in the bunny and help him guide the princess safely back to her bed.

FINISH

START

Aurora's friends are pretending to be her dance partner. Use your stickers to put them in order from biggest to smallest.

Who will join Jasmine on her next adventure? Imagine the scene using your stickers.

Where is Lumiere hiding?
Find and mark him with a sticker. Then, finish
coloring in the castle candelabras.

How many place settings does
Mrs. Potts have? Mark all the places where
the sequence appears in the grid's horizontal
lines with a cupcake sticker.

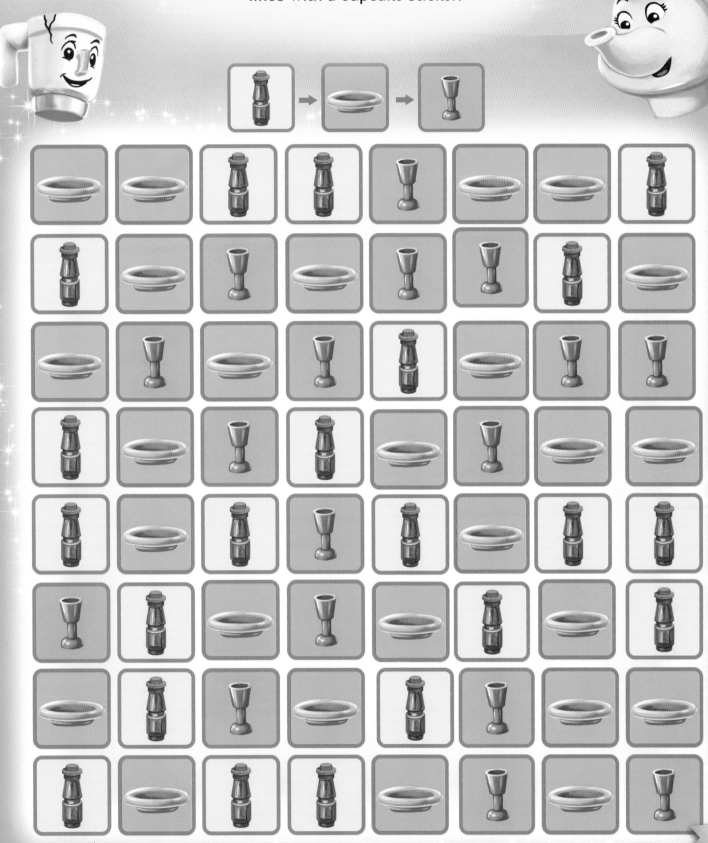

Stick in the musical objects next to
each member of Ariel's underwater band.

Color in the picture to see who
Ariel has spotted in her telescope.

Find the objects below and mark
them with red flower stickers.

Help Rapunzel and Pascal
draw a mural on her bedroom wall.
Then add stickers!

Use the coordinates below and
mark the flight path of the cupcake
on the grid with stickers.

C-1        B-2        C-3        D-4

|     | 1 | 2 | 3 | 4 |
|-----|---|---|---|---|
| A   |   |   |   |   |
| B   |   |   |   |   |
| C   |   |   |   |   |
| D   |   |   |   |   |

Which small picture of
Mulan matches the big picture?
Stick a fan sticker on it.

Which animals don't have
a matching partner at Snow White's forest party?
Mark them with purple flower stickers.

Stick in Snow White's guests in the empty spaces. Then, draw two straight lines to divide the apples into three groups, so the princess and her two friends get three apples each!

Match Tiana's friends' stickers to their shadows, then find them in the mess of animal outlines below.

Complete the grid with stickers,
so that there are four different things
in each row and column.

Decorate Cinderella's carriage by
continuing the pretty wheel patterns.

Find eight things that don't belong in Cinderella's palace. Mark them with blue bow stickers.

Aurora loves to spend time
outdoors! Create a fairy-tale scene
for her using your stickers.

Find the real Aladdin by matching
his shadow to one of the images below.
Mark him with a lamp sticker.

Follow the pattern to find a flight path
for Jasmine, moving only horizontally and vertically.
Mark the path with your stickers.

START

FINISH

Dinner is served! Stick Mrs. Potts
and Chip in the middle of the maze and help
everyone find their way to them.

The fastest path to Belle has the
most pictures of her. Add all the portrait stickers
and mark the winner with a rose sticker.

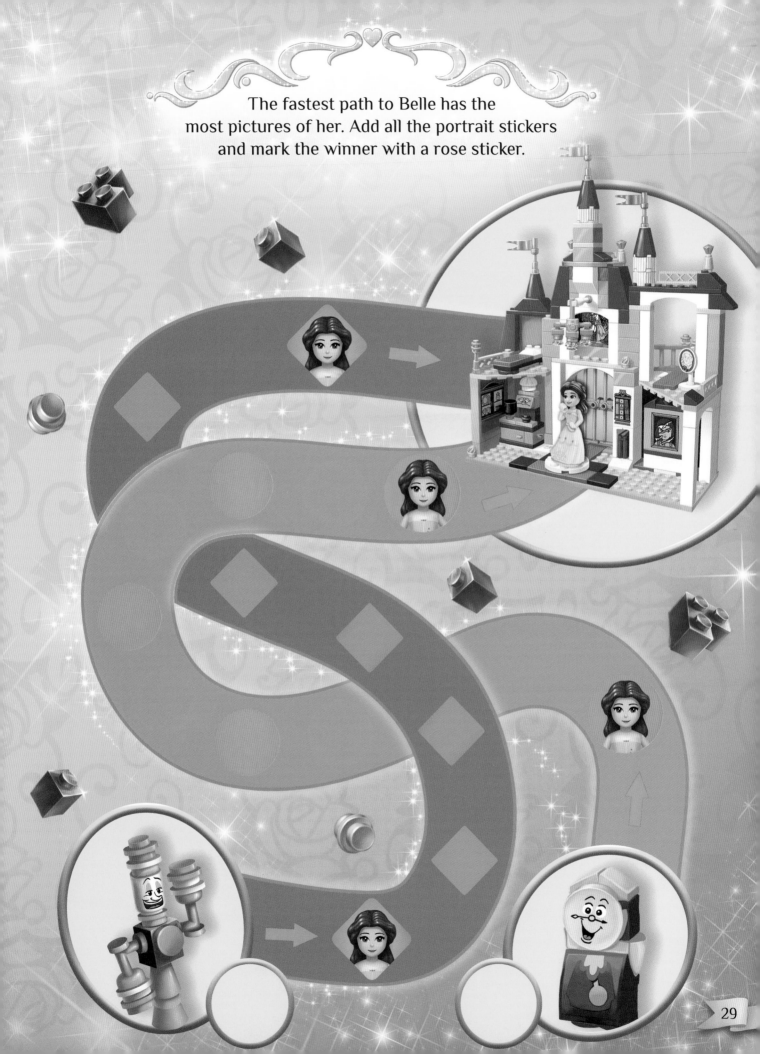

Ariel loves collecting things that people leave behind. Find the objects and mark them with trident stickers.

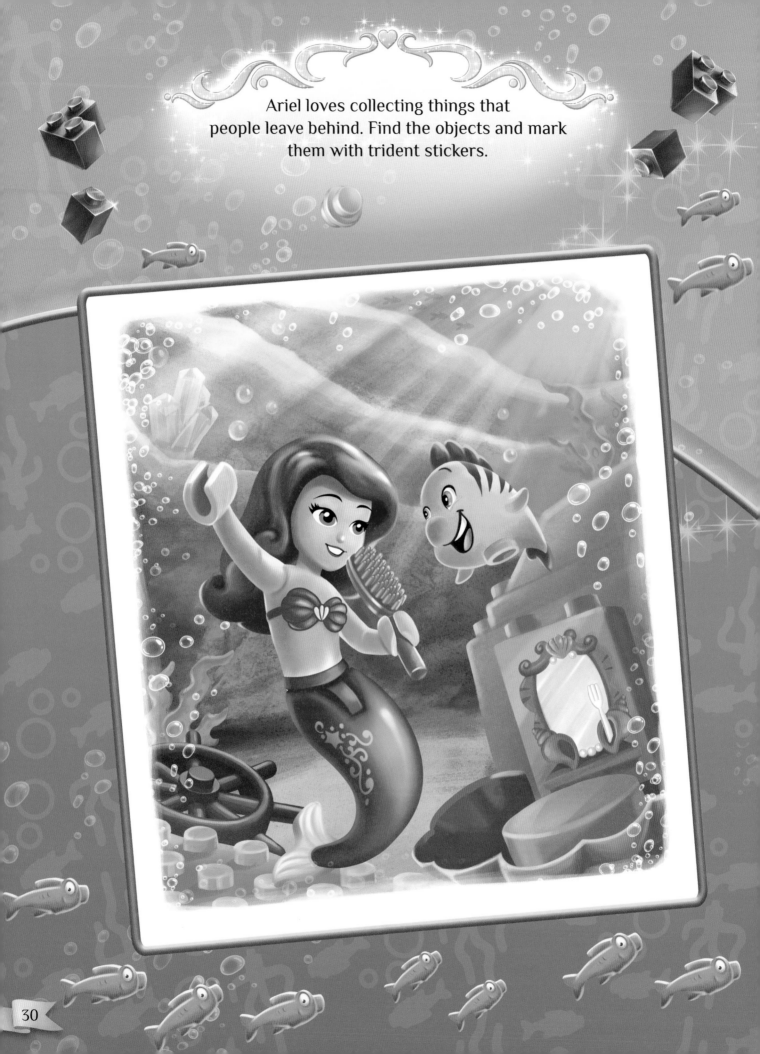

Ariel wants to build a doghouse
for Max. Add numbers to the circles to complete
the build. Stick in a bone for Max too!

Use your stickers to help
Rapunzel enjoy her day with
Pascal and Maximus.

WANTED

In every box there's an odd object.
Cover each of them with stickers
of the right objects.

Use pink flower stickers to mark six differences between the scene and its reflection in the water.

34

Complete the grid with stickers
so that no fan, pot, or cup is repeated
in any column or row.

Can you spot five birds hiding
in the picture below? Color in the picture
and use your stickers to mark them.

Lead Snow White through the trees
to the cottage. When you reach it, stick in
a tasty treat for the princess.

FINISH

START

37

Color in Tiana and the animals.
What has everyone had to eat? Match the
colored circles to find out.

Find five differences between
Tiana's portraits. Mark them with
your cookie stickers.

Find the small details in the big picture.
Mark them with heart stickers.

Follow the ribbons and mark who can
reach the glass slipper with a slipper sticker.

Which animals are missing
from the spinning wheel? Complete the
pattern with stickers.

In each row, what order do the
dresses appear in? Add stickers to complete
the rows. Then color in Aurora.

Use stickers to finish the puzzle and
discover what Jasmine's magic carpet looks like.

Using the top LEGO bricks, help Jasmine make three palm trees like the one in the circle. Which piece from the bottom row do you need to complete them? Mark it with a lamp sticker.

Belle is organizing her library. Figure out her pattern and put the book stickers in the empty spaces.

Draw the other half of the enchanted
rose and color in the flower

Mark the odd one out in each group with a turtle sticker.

Draw a line along Ariel's path
without touching the sides of it. Add a hairbrush
sticker to Ariel's throne, too!

Move along the arrows to the finish
by only going between neighboring flower
shapes that contain an identical object.

START

FINISH

Rapunzel spends a lot of time in her tower. Use your stickers to make her day more fun!

51

Set up a training area for Mulan
so she can sharpen her skills.

Which mirror image on the left matches
Snow White on the right? Color it in.

Snow White has surprise visitors!
Create a picnic scene with your stickers.

Connect the dots to see what dish
Tiana is cooking up in her restaurant.

Help Tiana find the frog that is
identical to the one she is holding, and
mark it with a crown sticker.

The mice are playing
hide-and-seek. Use your stickers to help them
hide behind the objects shown in the box.

Put the story of Cinderella's amazing adventure in the right order by writing the numbers 1-4 in the circles.

Mark five differences in
these pictures of Aurora's castle
with flower stickers.

What did Aurora put on her bed?
Look at the impression marks on the sheets
and add stickers of the right objects.

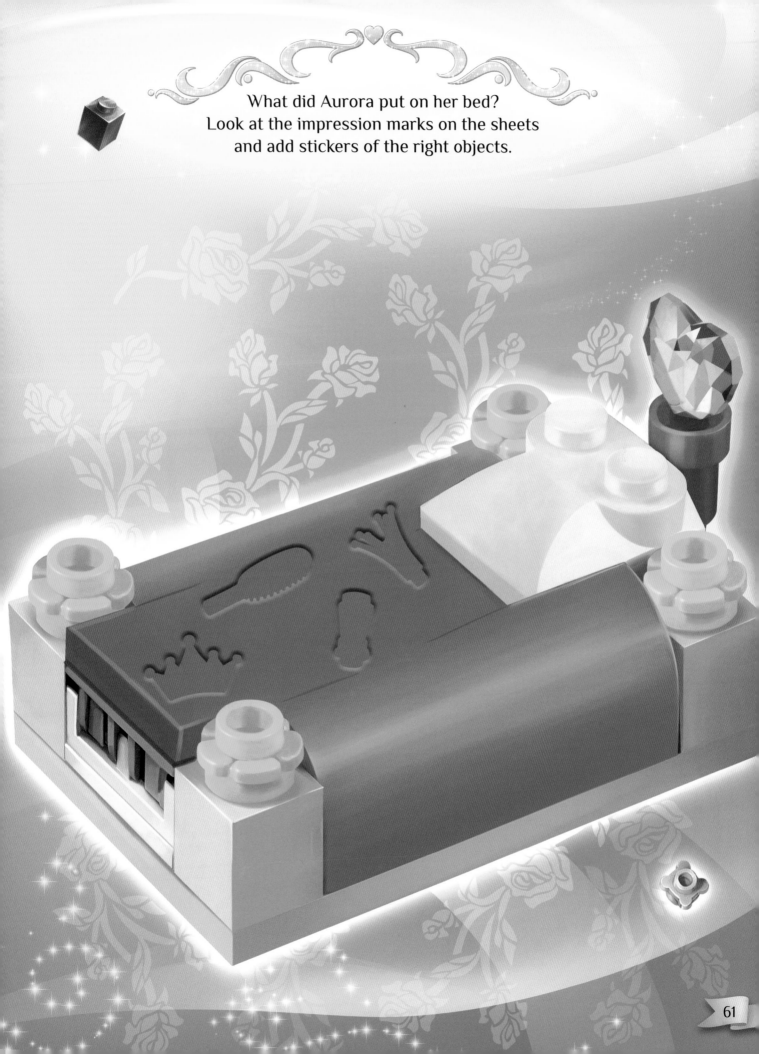

Follow the lines to see where
Jasmine's bird has decided to land.
Mark the spot with a bird sticker.

Find two chairs that
are exactly the same and mark
them with Rajah stickers.

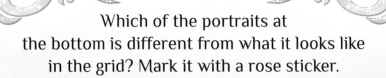

Which of the portraits at
the bottom is different from what it looks like
in the grid? Mark it with a rose sticker.

Help Belle organize her
wardrobe by sticking in the missing gloves
so that each of them has a pair.

Use your stickers to design
a fabulous floating party for Ariel!

## Learn how to draw Pascal.

### 1. Draw an oval.

### 2. Add a circle.

### 3. Add a curly tail.

### 4. Add arms and legs.

### 5. Add a big eye and a mouth.

Practice here!

Guide Mulan through the maze to the cherry tree.

START

FINISH

Balance Mulan's water buckets
by adding the correct number of water
stickers to the left bucket.

Cinderella's carriage is missing some parts! Put the stickers in the right places to fix it.

Mark all the things that
are in the picture of Lucifer's party
with your yellow flower stickers.

Stick in Aurora's animal friends
so that each one has a pair.

Which crown is identical
to the one Aurora is wearing below?
Mark it with a pink flower sticker.

On each market stall shelf,
there's an odd object. Mark it with
a pink crystal sticker.

Which shadow shape
matches Jasmine's palace at sunset?
Mark it with a Rajah sticker.

Use your stickers to create
a magical scene at Belle's castle!

Ariel is adding a slide to her castle!
Place a shell sticker next to the slide shape
that will land in the water.

START

Follow the pattern in the grid's horizontal and vertical lines to get to Ariel's underwater castle. Mark the path with stickers for Ariel's friends to follow.

FINISH

81

In what order should Mulan pick up her swords? Remember: she should start with the one lying on the top of the pile. Mark the last sword with a red apple sticker.

Which one of the small pictures
of Mulan is different from the others?
Find it and then use it as an example
to color in the big one.

Untangle the tracks to find
a path Cinderella and the Prince can dance
along without bumping into anything!

Mark the ball invitation that matches the one Cinderella is thinking about with a blue bow sticker.

Which picture piece
can't be found in the big picture?
Mark it with a bunny sticker.

Place the same number of blue, pink, purple, and red flowers on each of the bushes on either side of Aurora's castle.

Complete the drawing of
Khan—Mulan's loyal horse and friend.
Then color him and the princess in.

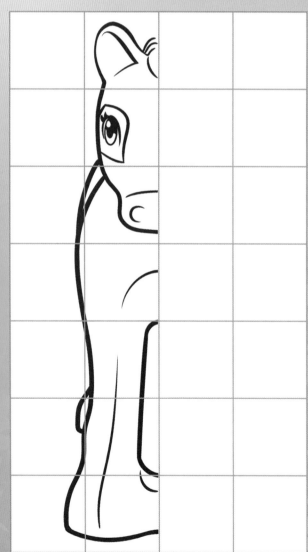

Mulan spends most of her spare
time training. Find this picture's exact copy.
Mark it with a sticker of Khan.

Ariel found a chest full of treasure!
Guide her boat along the white waves back
to the castle. Add a crown sticker at the finish.

START

FINISH

Look at the small picture below
and make a copy using your stickers.

Help Cinderella find her way
to Lucifer. When you reach the cat, place
a cheese sticker next to him.

Cinderella's carriage is ready
to take her to the ball! Use your stickers
to create an enchanting sunset.

# ANSWERS

p. 6

p. 7

p. 10
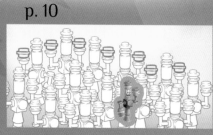

p. 11

p. 12

p. 13

p. 14

p. 16
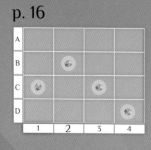

p. 17
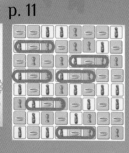

p. 18

p. 19

p. 20

p. 21

p. 23

p. 26

p. 27
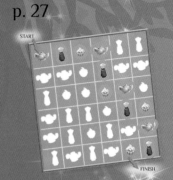

p. 28

p. 29

p. 30

p. 31
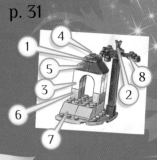

p. 33

p. 34

p. 35

# ANSWERS

p. 36

p. 37

p. 38

p. 39

p. 40

p. 41

p. 42

p. 43

p. 44

p. 45

p. 46

p. 48

p. 50

p. 54

p. 56

p. 57

p. 58

p. 59

p. 60

p. 61

p. 62

p. 63

# ANSWERS

p. 64

p. 65

p. 70

p. 71

p. 72

p. 73

p. 74

p. 75

p. 76

p. 77
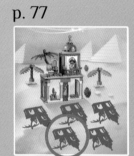

p. 80

p. 81
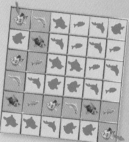

p. 82

p. 83

p. 84

p. 85

p. 86

p. 87

p. 89

p. 90

p. 91

p. 92

4-5

6

7

10

8-9

11

12

14

16

17

15

18

19

20

21

23

24-25

26

27

28

30

29

31

32

33

34

35

37

39

36

52-53

55

58

57

60

61

62

63

64

65

66-67

71

72

73

74

75

76

77

78-79

80

81

82

85

86

87

88

89

90

91

92

93